This is Mary Louise Edward's third novel. She has really allowed herself to find a way of making her characters come alive in her stories. She has the ability to allow the reader to capture, feel, and really relate to what her characters are about. She has had great opportunities to travel and live in all parts of the country. She currently resides in the Midwest and is working on her fourth novel.

This book is dedicated to Chris S., thanks for the inspiration you've given me for writing this wonderful story.

Mary Louise Edwards

A FORBIDDEN LOVE AFFAIR

AUSTIN MACAULEY PUBLISHERS™

LONDON • CAMBRIDGE • NEW YORK • SHARJAH

Ordering Information:
Quantity sales: special discounts are available on quantity purchases by corporations, associations, and others. For details, contact the publisher at the address below.

Publisher's Cataloguing-in-Publication data
Edwards, Mary Louise
A Forbidden Love Affair

ISBN 9781641823920 (Paperback)
ISBN 9781641823937 (Hardback)
ISBN 9781641823944 (ePub e-book)

Library of Congress Control Number: 2020908319

www.austinmacauley.com/us

First Published (2020)
Austin Macauley Publishers LLC
40 Wall Street, 28th Floor
New York, NY 10005
USA

mail-usa@austinmacauley.com
+1 (646) 5125767

Table of Contents

Chapter 1

It's that time of year once again with football season starting and racing still going on; businesses have been very busy. Craig had his hands full with tryouts and filling the new roster for the new playing season. Up north in Indianapolis, Heather was preparing her schedule for interviewing the coaches as well as the players for both college and professional football teams. She also had the privilege of interviewing the racecar drivers including her longtime boyfriend of five years, Kip Baxter. He had one hell of a record last season and this time he hoped to win this year and take home the cup. Heather had been a sportscaster for almost ten years now and she loves what she does. She had been a huge sports fan since she was a child growing up watching it with her father and his friends. Craig and Heather already knew each other from prior interviews and sports meetings. Somehow something seemed different this time; they both have a great deal of respect for one another. Craig's wife, Dana was a criminal defense attorney and they have a teenage daughter and been married now for 15 years. Craig also had a son from a prior marriage and sometimes had problems with him.

As for Heather, she doesn't have any children and the subject had never been discussed, not even marriage. They weren't living together and both agreed it was for the best due to their crazy lifestyles. They were both very busy with their jobs and both felt neither one needed any more stress added to their lives. Heather was now in South Bend for a few days covering the pre-game season. She was going to be speaking with Craig along with some of his players. After she wrapped things up with interviewing those that she could, she went back to her hotel room.

Heather knew that she would be in town for a couple days to finish up with the interviews. Since it was still early, she decided to go have a drink and relax. South Bend being an Irish town, there were a lot of Irish pubs downtown especially with it having one of the most popular colleges as well as football team, Notre Dame, also known as the Fighting Irish and one of the toughest catholic schools to get accepted into. As she walked into the pub, she noticed how packed it was. She approached the bar to get herself a drink and Craig and a few of friends were sitting across from where she was standing.

He noticed her right away and with a big smile on his face, his eyes lit up brightly, he stumbled with his words talking to them. They laughed at him and knew he was into Heather; it was really hard to hide it by the way he looked at her. Heather got her drink and began to walk through the crowd searching for a place to sit. Craig stood up and went to approach her and invited her to sit with him and his friends. "Heather…hi, it's nice to see you. Would you like to join me and my friends or are you here with someone?" Craig asked her and he was really hoping that she was alone and that she would agree to join him. He was saying to himself please be alone and come be with me.

She smiled as she was pleased to see him as well. "Hi, Craig, no I'm here alone and yes, I'd love to join you. I'm actually glad to see you, it's always awkward going into a strange place alone," she said to him.

"I know what you mean, so how long are you in town for?" he asked her as they walked back to his table.

"Only for two more days, I still have a lot of work to do.

Some follow up interviews to finish before heading back home," she said to him.

As they continued talking, there was something else going on and neither one was seeing it just yet. They were having such a great time and he grabbed her by the hand and pulled her out to the dance floor. Craig and Heather danced the rest of that night and these two had a great time being together. They talked about anything and everything and by the end of the night, they exchanged phone numbers. She then went back to her hotel room and he headed home for the night.

The next few nights, Craig had seemed different, he was smiling and happy and didn't seem so stressed and unhappy as usual. Heather had finished up her interviews and packed up to head back home to Indianapolis. Though, she wasn't even close to being done, as she had to prepare to interview the racecar drivers at the Indy Speedway. As she was driving back home, she couldn't help to think about that night with Craig. She hadn't danced like that in such a very long time or even had that much fun. As she thought about it, she couldn't remember the last time her and Kip had done anything like that together. Later that night as she was sitting in her office at her home going over a few things, Craig had called.

She was surprised that he called her and hearing his voice somehow made her feel nervous and yet excited. They spoke for hours that night and before letting her go, Craig asked her if he could see her again. He knew that it was wrong and crazy but there was just something about her and the way he felt when he was with her. Heather wasn't really sure about seeing him again but she couldn't help the way it felt being with him.

She also didn't want to jeopardize her career either if something bad were to happen between them. "Craig, this is crazy. We shouldn't even be thinking about seeing each other. I have a boyfriend who I really care for and you're married, too. I don't want anything to backfire and go wrong and I lose my job over this. I can't afford to mess up my career over something like this," she said to him.

Craig had understood everything that she had said and wasn't about to let that happen to either one of them. "I understand all of that Heather and I would not allow that to happen. I have my career to worry about also and well with my marriage; I'm a big boy and can take care of myself. Look, I understand if you don't want to see me outside of work; but I feel that we owe it to ourselves to figure out what's going on here," he said to her.

It was silent for a moment as Heather was thinking about what he had said. "I agree, there is definitely something going on here I just hope you're right about this Craig? I know I haven't had that much fun in such a long time; and can't even remember the last time Kip and I had done anything together," she was telling him. He knew what she meant and how she had felt.

"I know how you feel there, I couldn't tell you the last time Dana and I had done anything together alone or even with our daughter," he said to her.

They went on talking and ended up making plans to meet that following week. Craig was finding himself thinking about Heather more and more each day. Heather had got called away on an interview and had to cancel with Craig and then Kip had arrived at her home to see her. She was beginning to think that this was a sign for her to not get involved with Craig. But then something wasn't feeling right with Kip, something was off and she couldn't figure out what it could be. She wanted to see if their relationship was even worth carrying out since she felt it wasn't going anywhere. All they did it seemed was work and never do anything together but talk about work and she didn't want that all the time. She wanted to be able to have something real with Kip and it was starting to feel like all they had was a work relationship instead of a romantic one. Heather decided it was time to say something to Kip about it and see what happens. After talking with Kip about them doing something together, he had actually agreed and even apologized for ignoring her. She knew that this was a busy time for him as it was for her. Not long after Kip had left and went home for the night, Craig had sent Heather a text message. He told her that he was having a bit of a problem and that was he couldn't seem to stop thinking about her. She smiled and laughed as she read his message and she replied back to him. She let him know that she had made plans with Kip to do something and she was hoping to save her relationship. She let him know that she needed to know how things were going to go between them first. Craig texted back that he understood and agreed, then told her that he would wait for her to let him know when she wanted to see him.

Craig was really hoping that things didn't work out between them and he couldn't believe he was feeling that way. He thought how he could think that way when he was married to where she was only dating someone. He continued on with his normal activities and he stayed very busy between practices and games. Over the next several days, Heather was spending a lot of time with Kip and even though she enjoyed herself, she was realizing that it wasn't the same. She had devoted the last five years of her life to this guy and from the beginning of their relationship, they had already set down ground rules and boundaries. Right away without even realizing it, they were in a business relationship not a loving romantic one.

They hardly ever went out together or had any real fun together, it was always about work and what needed to be done. Heather knew that was not the kind of relationship that she wanted with someone she was supposed to care for and love. Kip never wanted to stay the whole night and be with her and he always seemed to be pre-occupied about something. Heather decided to back off and leave things alone for a while and see what happened next. She let Kip know how she had felt and her concerns about their relationship. He had got upset over it and told her she was reading too much into things. Everything seemed to be falling apart for Heather as she wasn't for sure what was going on between her and Kip.

However, right now wasn't the time to be worrying about it because she had to work. This was the busiest time for her as she had to interview team players and then discuss sports on the network. While she was discussing plays how the teams were doing in both divisions, she couldn't help to think about Craig. It seemed as if these two had the same minds because he was thinking about her too and even watching her on television. He always kept up to date with what's going on with the news and the sports reviews. He wanted so badly to call her and hear her voice again on the phone instead of hearing her on television. It just made him want to see her even more and he knew it was wrong but he couldn't help himself. Craig had been staying later than usual working in his playbook trying to make sure he didn't miss anything and had everything organized for each practice and game. He was realizing that his wife had even stopped asking him to join her to go to bed.

She had been very busy with her cases and working late and sometimes she wouldn't get home until late in the evening or late at night. Then take care of their daughter and go to bed without even saying anything to him. At first, it didn't bother him because he never thought anything of it until recently and now it was making him think things. He thought that his marriage might be in trouble too and didn't even think of anything until now.

Of course, with him wanting to see Heather wasn't a good sign either and the way she had made him feel had him questioning things. Craig had decided to do something that he knew might be a mistake but he didn't care, he needed to see Heather. So, he finished up for the day and drove up to Indianapolis and went to the news station where she worked. He walked inside and went to the studio and they allowed him to watch her finish up her show. When she got done and left to go to her room, she noticed him standing by the camera crew. She smiled and he smiled back at her. "What are you doing here?" she asked him.

"I had to see you; I hope you're not mad?" he said to her.

She shook her head and smiled. "No. I'm not mad just surprised is all," she said to him.

"Great. Wow, you look great. Are you hungry? Do you have time to be with me?" he asked her.

"Thanks. Yes, I could use a bite to eat. What did you have in mind?" she said to him.

He looked at her and smiled. "I don't really care where we eat; I just want to be with you, Heather. I can't believe this but I've missed you. Is that wrong to have missed someone you barely know?" he said to her.

She looked at him. "Well I wouldn't say we barely know each other, we have worked together for many years, Craig. We just never personally got to know one another and to answer your question, no it's not wrong at all. It's nice to know you have people out there who care enough about you to miss you," she said to him.

He looked at her and grinned. "Well, then we need to do something about it then. Because I really like you and plan to get to know you, if that's all right with you?" he said to her.

As they left the studio, she had him follow her to her place to drop her car off, that way she could ride with him. He liked that because now he knew where she lived in case, he ever wanted to visit her some time. Craig had felt that it would take time to see where this went between them and right now, he just wanted to be with her and really get to know who she was. They both also knew that they had to be extremely careful so nobody found out or caught them together outside of work. They both had a great deal of respect for one another and wasn't about to cost one another their careers. This wasn't going to be easy for either of them if anything began to develop between them. They had a great dinner and laughed and talked for hours and it was getting late so he took her back to her house and walked her to her door. He had to give her a proper goodbye and before leaving her, he gently kissed her on the lips and when his lips met hers, it was like fireworks going off. He looked into her eyes and couldn't believe the feeling he had felt. She had felt it too and it scared her because she knew this was not going to be a good thing.

Nothing was said as he turned and walked away from her. Craig had left and went back home thinking about that kiss and how he wanted to do it again. All she could do was go inside and take her a long hot bath and think about what she was getting herself into and if it was really worth it. It was very late when he got home that night, nothing was said because his wife was already in bed asleep. With that, he decided to just go to bed for the night. He knew that he had a long week ahead of him and he needed to have his head straight and be focused for their first game.

Though, he knew he couldn't keep from thinking about Heather and he didn't want to either. All he knew was this was going to be the start of a great season and he was ready for anything, especially if it was being with Heather.

As the weeks had passed by, Craig began to realize just how unhappy he had been. He couldn't think when the last time he had made love to his wife or the last time he had shared their bed. For the last several months now, he had been sleeping on the sofa. At first it started out that way because he didn't want to wake her up when he got home late at night. Then it just became a routine since she had never said anything to him or even tried waking him up to join her in bed. They both had very busy careers that kept them on the road traveling or at the office until late in the morning.

Craig was missing his wife and missing what they once had together. Now he was becoming very lonely and longing to be held and touched and even loved but somehow, he lost that need with her. He didn't know how to try with her anymore and he had felt as if he may not even want the life he once had with his wife. They were now strangers living in the same house raising their daughter together. That was the last thing that Craig had wanted but he knew he couldn't continue living that way. He hated how he was thinking about cheating but every time he was with Heather, it seemed to feel more right than it was wrong. Craig would catch himself thinking about her more than he should and wondering how it might be to hold her in his arms all night long. However, he knew how bad it could all turn out if he were to cheat on his wife. He began to stay focused on his daughter and what it would do to her and his career that he loved so much. After thinking about it, he decided it was best to think about what was at stake here. So, with that he was going to try and not give in and be with Heather. He thought that he owed it to himself to at least try to save his marriage first. It was very late that night so he decided to sleep in their bedroom and wait for Dana to get home. It was time to do something, he had thought as he got undressed and crawled into bed.

As Craig reached over to hold her and began kissing on her, she asked him what he was doing. He sat up and told her that he would like to make love to her. She was very cold and distant towards him. "It's very late, Craig, and I'm very tired and have to be up very early in the morning."

She said to him. He shakes his head in disbelief and lies back down. "That has never stopped you before, but okay, sorry for wanting to make love to my wife," he says to her. He turned his back to her not understanding what had happened to them. Then he started to think about Heather and how it would feel for once to be with someone who actually wanted to be with him.

Chapter 2

A few days later, Heather had wrapped up her interviews and assignments for the night. Kip had surprised her and they went out for a late dinner. That night after they had returned back to her place, Heather began to light up some candles and then put on a long pajama shirt. Kip was sitting on the sofa and while he was searching for a movie to watch, she sat next to him and began to kiss on his neck. Without thinking, he pulled away and looked at her in a funny way. "What are you doing, Heather?" he asked her. She looked at him and backed away from him.

"I was hoping that maybe we could spend some time together, Kip. It's been awhile since we've made love and I've missed you," she said to him. He knew at that moment that he needed to explain to her why he had been distant and avoiding making love to her.

"Heather, there's something that I need to tell you and I just hope you don't hate me afterwards," he said to her. She could see the fear in his eyes and knew that it must be something serious.

"Of course not, Kip, whatever it is, we can work it out. What's wrong?" she said to him.

Kip knew that it wasn't fair to keep his secret from her any longer as she didn't deserve to be in relationship that wasn't going anywhere. "Look, there is a reason why I have been distant towards you and not wanting to have sex with you," he said to her and she could tell it was very hard for him by his actions.

"Is there someone else, Kip?" she asked him. He looked at her with hurt in his eyes.

He never wanted to hurt her at all, but he knew he couldn't continue keeping her wondering what was wrong. "Yes. It's not what you think though, there is not another woman, Heather. It's a guy, my parents would disown me and my career would be over with if anyone knew. I'm so sorry, I never wanted to hurt you at all. Heather, you're my best friend. You mean so much to me and I do love you very much, just not romantically. I hope you can forgive me and not hate me for this?" he said to her. She looked at him and leaned over to hug him and assured him that she couldn't hate him. They spent the evening watching movies and she had agreed to keep his secret and be his pretending girlfriend until he was ready to reveal his secret.

Though, she was a little saddened by it but also knew that it was for the best because she had been thinking a lot about Craig lately. She had spoken about him to Kip and then he told her about his boyfriend and how happy he was to finally meet someone other than her that he could connect with. Then Kip had promised her that if she found someone that she wanted to be with and really cared for; they'd tell everyone that they ended the relationship. They agreed that they would remain friends. Heather loved that plan and as it got late into the night, he decided to sleep over and she went to her bedroom and went to bed. By early morning, Kip was up and gone and Heather didn't have to work that day. She decided to get caught up on the household chores. As she cleaned her house, all she could think about was Craig and she knew how wrong that was and she thought maybe she should leave him alone. She began working on a few assignments and preparing notes for upcoming interviews.

She didn't have a full line-up and hasn't been able to interview everyone with everything going on. With working in sports, she had the opportunity of traveling and interviewing both of the team players. Heather was very busy but she loved her job and had the opportunity to see all the games. This was the same when she would interview the racecar drivers from both NASCAR and Indy race teams.

Meanwhile, Craig wasn't too happy with Dana at all as he was getting very upset with her, constantly ignoring him and neglecting to spend any time with him. They both worked stressful long hours, he knew that but he was still missing his wife and it seemed as if she didn't want anything to do anymore. It was beginning to feel as if they were roommates, now strangers raising their teenage daughter. He had some time off and he was planning on doing something with both his daughter and wife. However, when he shared his plans with Dana about what he wanted to do, she just shook her head. "Craig, I'm sorry but I just have too much going on right now especially with this new case I'm working on. It's not a good time to be planning anything right now," she said to him.

Craig couldn't believe what he was hearing and this time he was done trying to do anything with her. "Dana, what is going on? Why are you constantly avoiding me and not want to be with me?" he asked her.

"I don't really know right now, Craig. I think that maybe we've just grown apart from our busy careers. I'm sorry but maybe we both need to really think about things," Dana said to him.

He couldn't believe what he was hearing from her. "Are you serious? Do you hear what you're saying, Dana? We are supposed to be a family, we have a marriage and our daughter, what about that? I have been trying to spend time with you and have the three of us go somewhere. You keep pushing me away and saying we are too busy and that's just all bullshit! I'm tired of having to be alone and not being able to make love to my wife or spend time with you. I need to know what it's going to be so I know what to do," Craig said to her.

She couldn't believe the way he was acting and what he was saying to her. She really had no answers for him because she knew it was over and she wasn't ready to walk away just yet. "I'm sorry that you feel this way, Craig, but right now I think it is best that we talk about this another time. I have a lot to get done tonight and prepare for my case tomorrow. So please understand that I am aware that you have some concerns and we will talk next week," she said to him as she went to her office down the hall. Craig again was in disbelief of her and how she could be so cold to him. This was it, he thought and he knew that it was over as he could feel it. As he walked away, all he could think about was his daughter and what it would do to her if he decided to walk away now.

Craig knew that he couldn't keep living his life like this, he needed someone to love him and he could love back. He wanted to call Heather right then at that moment and talk with her and just hearing her voice again made him very happy. While he was in bed watching the sports channel, he grabbed his phone and called her. At this point now, he didn't care anymore and if anyone said anything, he would just let them think it was business. Heather was very pleased to hear from him and they spoke for an hour that night. It made him feel great talking with her about everything and then they made plans to get together that week.

Craig felt if his own wife didn't want to be with him, then he would be with someone who actually did. That night as Craig spoke with Heather, he told her how he felt that there was nothing left in his marriage. She could hear the hurt in his voice as she listened to him. He went on to tell her how they don't even have a real relationship; and how she's always making excuses why she can't be with him. After telling her all of that, he realized that he may have said too much. He didn't want to involve her in his marital problems, even though he was starting to care for her.

Craig was very stressed out over everything and he didn't want to burden Heather with his problems. Even though, Heather had assured him that it was alright to talk with her. Craig was still uneasy about it. They finished talking that night and he went to sleep knowing that he had a lot to figure out. Now Dana had begun to sense things and now regrets her actions for ignoring him the way she had. With Craig completely ignoring her unless it concerned their daughter, it has left her feeling the worse. Though, he had stopped trying to be with her and moved on to spend his time with Heather, he had no intentions on leaving his wife. Dana had decided to try and make up for everything by planning a romantic evening and dinner for the two of them. She didn't think to call him to let him know as she wanted to surprise him for when he got home that evening.

This left Dana sitting, waiting until the late hours of that night. When she realized Craig wasn't coming any time soon, she decided to clean up for the night and put everything away. Not knowing what to really do at this point or how to think or feel, she sat there at the table thinking about things. Days later and their house had never been as cold as it had been lately. Dana wasn't about to keep quiet any longer, she was sensing that he may be seeing someone now.

With the way that she had neglected him, she really couldn't blame him if he was. Though, she was praying that wasn't the case and that he was just very hurt and keeping his distance from her. While on her lunch break, she decided to call Craig about making plans for the weekend. Craig was very much surprised by the call from her and thought it would be nice to be together. He explained to her that he was in a very important meeting and would see her when he got home. After talking with Dana, he thought it was odd of her to suddenly want to spend time together. A part of him was missing his family and missing what he once had with Dana.

Although, now he had grown to care deeply for Heather, which of course, had him in one hell of a bad mess. Hours later, Craig called to speak with Heather about spending the weekend with his wife and daughter. She understood and let him know that he needed to do what he felt needed to be done. Heather cared a lot for him and she knew what was at risk when she got involved with him. Craig was very surprised with how she was handling this situation because he was actually having a hard time. "I want you to know that I have grown to care deeply for you, Heather. You have become a very important part of my life and a very good friend to me," Craig said to her.

"I care greatly for you too, Craig, but you are married and I knew what I was getting into. I hope you know that nothing changes with us being friends if things work out for you and wife," Heather said to him.

This was killing him inside now because now he didn't know how he would feel after being with his wife again. It had been so long since he had made love to his wife and less than a month being with Heather. Heather knew that it wouldn't be easy to let him go but she was prepared to step back and allow him the chance to save his marriage. "I appreciate that, Heather. I really do but something like this just isn't easy to stop and walk away from. I really care for you and maybe even love you now. I can't just turn my feelings on and off like a switch it just doesn't work. Hell, right now I don't even know how I really about my wife, which is why I need to find out by being with her this weekend," he said to her. Heather couldn't believe what she had heard from him that he may love her. She wasn't about to question it or say anything as she just listened to him. They spoke for a while longer and then went on about their day.

It's Friday and Dana had some very interesting plans for them that evening. As Craig was finishing up; at the college he begins thinking about how all this will turn out. He was concerned that he might not be able to be with Dana and she would find out about his involvement with Heather. Before he left that afternoon to go home, he decided to call Heather and talk with her. He had to hear her voice and make sure that things were good between them. She knew how he had felt and assured him that everything was good. Just hearing that and knowing that he wasn't going to lose her made him feel at ease.

Even though it was something that he knew he had to do and by being with his wife this weekend, he would know how he felt for her. Craig had went home not really knowing what to expect or how things would work out between them. Dana was home waiting for him and she had an evening planned for them: which was to go out for dinner and maybe some dancing afterwards. Craig really wasn't up to dancing, at least not with her and even though he knew it was wrong to think that, it was how he had felt. Craig knew that too much time had passed and now they had become more like strangers. They both had drifted too far apart and his heart had found another to care for. Though, he stuck it out to make the best of things for the weekend. The only place he really wanted to be was with Heather and holding her in his arms.

Craig knew that he couldn't stop thinking about her, no matter how hard he tried. This was not good for Craig as he sat there talking with Dana; all he could see when he looked at her was Heathers' face. Craig didn't even realize that he had drifted off and wasn't paying any attention to Dana. It took her several times questioning him until she got his attention. Craig was unaware of it and played it off as things at work had been bothering him. He went on to keep his focus and attention on her while he was really thinking about Heather. Hours later, they were back home for the night and his only concern was that she didn't want to take it any further. He was really hoping that she didn't want to make love because he wasn't sure he could be with her. Well, he thought too soon as she grabbed him by the hand and began walking to their bedroom.

All he could think about now was he hoped not to say Heathers' name. She was all he could think about and it was going to take everything that he had to not say the wrong things. Craig looked at Dana as she slowly and easily removed her clothes. He still seen her as attractive but the real question now, was the love still there. Well, Craig was about to find out as he removed his clothes and approached her. There he was looking into her eyes and he leaned in to kiss her. It was like the first time with them all over again, only this time he was nervous for other reasons.

As they made love, Craig could feel there was nothing left anymore, the feeling was gone. Things were very different between them now. Dana could even feel something was different and it left her feeling concerned. Could their marriage be over after all these years? They were already like strangers as they have both neglected their marriage and allowed their relationship to fall apart.

Later that night, nothing was said as they just held each other and went to sleep for the night. Dana knew that she was mostly to blame as all she did was keep pushing him away instead of saying or doing something. Craig had felt very badly about this because he realized that even though he loved his wife; he had loved Heather more. This wasn't over as they had the whole weekend to spend together and Dana felt things would get better as they spent time together. As the weekend continued, they decided to take their daughter and have some family fun time. The tension was thick that even their daughter could sense something was wrong. Although, she had already known that her parents were having problems as they barely spoke or did anything together like they used to. These two days were good and it opened both of their eyes to see that they had some problems. Something needed to be done and now was the time to do something about it.

So, later that night they decided to really talk and lay everything out to be discussed. They both knew that they had a long way to go and now the question was if their marriage was worth saving? Craig had a lot of difficult decisions to make with some tough choices. Would he be able to give up Heather and walk from her to save his marriage with Dana? Did he even want to let her go and walk away from someone who he knew really cared for him? Craig was faced with some very difficult choices and decisions and now he had to really think about what he wanted. Of course, he knew he just couldn't walk away and leave his wife as they had their daughter. Dana had suggested that they attend marriage counseling to help them save their marriage.

Another thing was that, Craig had failed to mention his affair he had been involved in with Heather. There was no way in hell that he was going to involve Heather and cause problems for her. She had become a great friend to him and he was not about to lose that, no matter how all this turned out. He loved her very much and now he had to make sure that he kept her protected and safe from everything. It was already killing him that he had to hide and sneak off to call her or see her. He was now in way too deep and all he kept remembering was what had he said to her. He had told her one night how it was very frustrating because you can't turn feelings on and off like a switch.

He knew that he loved her, he knew it the moment he seen her walk in that bar and when they danced. Then when he made love to her the first time, he knew it and he melted in her kisses. Dana had set session appointments for them for counseling next month. All Craig could think about was wanting to be with Heather. He spoke with her about it later in the week and felt like he just wanted to end it and be with her. Heather flattered as she was by it reminded him what it would do to his daughter and that he also needed to do what was best for him. She informed him that she wasn't going to make him choose or get in the way of his marriage. Heather then had advised that it may be best for him to leave her alone and focus on his marriage. That was the last thing that Craig had wanted and now he feared that he could lose her now.

Craig needed to see Heather and speak with her in person and explain to her how he really felt. This something that couldn't wait and Heather agreed to see him. So with that, Craig made plans to see her that next afternoon. When Craig had got to her place, he was a nervous wreck and excited to see her. He had to explain to her that he was in love with her and he was afraid of losing her. Heather just listened to him as he poured out his heart to her and then he went on to explain she was more than just a friend. Craig had cheated on his first wife with his second wife and then two years after they were married, they had their daughter. He was young and a player, he admitted that and he really tried to make it work with Dana but they grew apart. He went on to tell her that it was different with her because he wasn't looking since he was married and loved his wife. He went to tell her how she made him feel alive and loved; that she was a friend which he hadn't had in a very long time. Heather had just realized that Craig really did love her more than she knew.

Chapter 3

Craig was now forced to make some serious decisions with his marriage and his own life. After thinking about what he wanted and needed to do, he had decided to stay with his wife. Craig began to play this out very delicately between rekindling his marriage with Dana and spending as much time as he could with Heather. He didn't want to lose Heather and if he left his wife, he would be tied up in a divorce and a custody battle that he didn't want. He felt it would be better to stay with Dana and be there with his daughter.

Heather was of course very uncomfortable with the situation; though she went along with it since she was now in too deep. She broke down and confided in her friend trying to decide what she should do. Although, she knew what needed to be done, it was deciding what she should do. Craig had assured her that he really did love her and he admitted that he had made a mess of his life. He was exhausted with always doing the right thing or what he felt was the right thing to do. Over the next several weeks, Craig and Dana begin to spend more time together.

Heather on the other hand had taken on more work as she was feeling very overwhelmed from everything. She thought about walking away from him completely and letting him go for good. As she knew she had no right to be with him, she still loved him and wasn't ready to give him up just yet. Heather was feeling so many things right now that she had decided it was time for a vacation. She needed to get away alone by herself to think about everything and figure out what to do without any distractions.

Heather decided to take a vacation to clear her head and pull her thoughts together. Even though, Craig was spending more time at home and with Dana; he couldn't stop thinking about Heather. He was missing her greatly and needed to hear her voice, so he decided to take a chance and call her. Craig walked into his office at home and called her late that night. Heather didn't answer, therefore, as he left her a message, Dana had overheard him talking on the phone. When he walked out of the room, she questioned him and he quickly informed her that it was about work and regarding one of his players.

Two days later, he hadn't heard from her and now he was concerned not knowing what was going on. Craig later called the T.V. station to see if she was working and they informed him she was on vacation. After finding out that she had taken her vacation and would be gone a week, he decided to take a day off work. He needed to find her and make sure things were good between them. He knew that he had himself tangled up in one hell of a mess and he wasn't about to lose Heather. Of course, Craig had thought about it so many times to just leave his wife to be with Heather. It didn't seem or feel real anymore between them, even with them trying to make things work.

Craig drove to Heathers' place that next day and discovers that she's not home and decides to sit outside her place and wait for her. After a few hours of waiting for her and her not showing up, he called her to see where she was. He also informed her that he was at her house hoping to see her. Heather answered this time only to let him know that she needed some time to be alone. She needed time to think about what she wanted and should do about everything. He could hear the hurt in her voice as she spoke to him.

He questioned her about not wanting to see him anymore, that he didn't want to lose her. "Heather, please don't leave me. I don't want to lose you; you know how I feel about you," he said to her.

"I don't want to lose you either, Craig; but it's not like I really have you, you're already taken. This isn't easy for me and the more I am with you, the more I care for you and want to be with you," she said to him.

"Believe me I understand, Heather. It's like I've said before, it's not like a switch you can turn on and off. I happen to feel the same way here and it has me scared that I am going to lose you," he said to her.

"Craig, I just need some time to get my thoughts together…get my head straight. I was in the middle of something, I will call you in a few days," she said to him. "Okay, I understand and I just want you to know that I will never hurt you intentionally. You're very special and very important to me, I want you to know that," he said to her.

She smiled and it felt good knowing that. "I know, Craig, and you're important to me too. Good-bye, Craig. I'll talk to you later," she said to him.

"Okay, bye Heather," he said to her. Heather was now an even bigger mess than before, but she knew that she couldn't stay away or ignore him forever. That wouldn't be fair to either of them with the way they both had felt for one another. Regardless, if it was wrong or right to be together, it was already too late as they both had feelings for each other.

Craig had gone right back to the way things were going before, he began trying to make things work with his wife. He started working regularly again and sleeping in the lower level of his house. He had a very busy fall this season and it seemed every year got busier. However, he did pay attention to his wife and took her out for lunch at times. He knew the last thing that he needed was for Dana to suspect anything.

He had even planned a dinner and had the table set for when she got home one night from work. Dana was very surprised with the candle light setting and the home-cooked meal. Craig had even set out a very nice bottle of wine for them and they enjoyed a nice romantic dinner that night. Heather had been very busy with interviewing sports teams and racecar drivers and such. It had been almost two months since they had seen one another, only a few phone calls here and there. All Craig could think about was getting Heather alone and making love to her all night long and holding her in his arms. A few nights ago, Craig and Dana were enjoying the evening and they started making out and kissing when Dana pulled away. She couldn't continue with this anymore either as she told Craig she was tired and went to bed. Craig had realized at that moment that he wasn't in love with her anymore. He couldn't get excited and he felt that she had felt the same way and just let him think she was tired.

As he went to bed that night, he felt somewhat relieved as now he may not have to try so hard anymore being his wife. Then a part of him felt bad because she was his wife and they had been married for fifteen years. He also had his daughter to think about but also knew that in four years, she would be gone to college. Now it seemed that things just might be different and he would have more time to spend with Heather.

Meanwhile, Heather had been spending some time with a friend from work. They had been out a few times on business dates and now she had been thinking about things. She loved Craig very much but she also knows she will never have anything real with him. Even if he did get divorced from his wife later, how could Heather ever fully trust him enough to want anything serious with him? Which had led her to believe that she needed to let him know how she felt and what she was really thinking. It was time to take their relationship to the next level with the truth of what they needed to accept and admit. Now, Heather was back in South Bend for work as usual and after the conferences were over, Craig pulled her aside. He was very happy to see her and she was excited to see him as well. He invited her out for dinner and drinks so they could catch up. She agreed and they left and went to a bar and grill. He couldn't keep his eyes off of her or stop from smiling at her. It didn't take them long to get caught up at all that evening and they spoke for hours. Craig couldn't wait to get her alone and kiss her soft sweet lips and hold her in his arms.

Craig informed her that his wife and his daughter were out of town for the week. He wanted to take Heather back to his house to spend some time with her. She wasn't very comfortable with going to his house as that was just disrespectful to his wife. Even though it was a sin just being with him, she knew she would pay for it later. It had been so long since she had seen him and she knew that she needed to talk with him. Heather agreed to go with him back to his place and she was very nervous over it. Craig was just happy having her with him and he knew he couldn't have her there too long. They had a few drinks and made love on his couch and afterwards took a shower together.

It was very magical and between all the sweating, he couldn't see the tears from her eyes. Heather knew she really loved him as they made love and couldn't help to cry from how she had felt. Heather felt it would be best not to talk about anything serious while she was in his home. It was too late, however, Craig was already feeling and sensing something was wrong with her. So, as they got dressed and went back to the couch, he questioned her. He wanted to know why she seemed to be upset and felt that it was because he brought her back to his place.

"Hey, is everything okay, you seem upset about something?" he asked her.

"Well, actually I was going to talk with you about it later but I guess now is as good as any," she said to him.

"Is something wrong, Heather?" he asked her.

Now was the time for everything to come out and be said, so she knew where to go from here and he knew how she really felt. Heather finally decided to tell Craig how she really felt about him. It was very hard for her since she just couldn't call him or see him whenever she wanted. She knew if she wanted to speak with him that she would have to wait until he was at the college. Well turns out that Craig had felt the same as he knew he couldn't just talk with her anytime or see her either. The waiting and anticipating was just overwhelming for them both. Craig had called her to see how she was doing and that was when she had to tell him how she felt. She also realized that this affair couldn't keep going on any longer.

"Craig, I don't think I can keep doing this…I really care for you and we both know this isn't going anywhere. Really to be honest I think its way past caring and more like I love you," she was telling him.

He already knew it. He could feel it as he told her that he really cared for her. Though, he couldn't tell her what she needed to hear, not yet anyway. "Heather, you know how I feel about you, you are very special to me and I do care deeply for you. I know this is hard for you because it's really hard for me. Damn, see this is what I was trying to tell you how this isn't something you can just turn on or off. In case you haven't noticed, I have come to really care for you as well. I spend more time with you than I have with my wife in almost year. I don't know what's going to happen, most likely end up getting a divorce after my daughter leaves for college. I can't say what will happen with anything but I do know that I have tried being with my wife and all I can think about is being with you," Craig had said to her with hurt in his voice and she could tell that he really cared and maybe even loved her.

Craig had fallen in love with Heather but he couldn't tell her he had felt that way. At least not yet anyway, it had to wait and he was not about to tell her over the phone. He went on to talk with her about renting a cabin and spending the weekend with her while they were away for the football game. Heather explains that she needed to think about that amongst other things. She needed to get her head straight and make her heart get on board with what should be done. Craig had let her know since his school is playing against Michigan State that he could get a nice quiet place for them away from everyone.

That evening, Heather had finished her shift at the station and a friend of hers whom also worked there approached her. His name was Brian Reynolds and he was a news reporter. He had asked her out for drinks and she gladly accepted as she knew she could use one or two. Now, Brian was a real character, always playing around and telling jokes and flirting with all the women. With everything going on, she had forgotten about helping Kip with keeping his secret of being gay. While she was out having drinks with Brian and deeply thinking about what she was going to do about Craig, Kip had called her. He needed to see her right away and it couldn't wait until the next day. Heather could tell something wasn't right so she assured him she was on her way to see him.

When Heather got to Kip's place, he was a mess and very upset with what had happened with him earlier that day. Kip's boyfriend had been involved with another man. He unexpectedly showed up at his boyfriend's place only to find him in bed with another man. Kip's boyfriend, who was Wayne Shayfield had been cheating on him and using him to get closer to another man. Anyway, he was heartbroken by this and Heather felt bad for him. As they sat there talking about failed relationships and how messing things can become, they decided to make a night of watching sappy movies and stuffing their faces with veggies and ice cream. Heather was still thinking about spending the weekend with Craig while they were away for the game.

However, she was also feeling as if she should get out while she still had some dignity left. Who was she kidding, she thought to herself as she knew Craig would never leave his wife and if he did, how could she fully trust him if they did get serious? Even though Heather knew how wrong it was to be with Craig, there was this whole other force keeping her from letting him go. As she watched movies with Kip, both crying over sappy romance movies, she got a phone call. Surprisingly, it was Craig so she quickly answered to see what he could possibly want this late at night. "Did I interrupt something, Heather? If so, I'm sorry I had to talk to you," Craig said to her.

"No. It's alright I'm watching movies with a friend. Is something wrong, are you okay?" Heather asked him.

"I just don't know what I'm going to do anymore. I've made a mess of things. I don't know who I am anymore; it seems like all I know how to do is destroy people's lives that care about me and I care for," he was saying to Heather. Heather felt as if he had been drinking by the way he was talking and by the sound of his voice.

"Craig, have you been drinking? Where are you right now?" she asked him.

"Yes, actually I have been drinking and I'm at home, sitting outside by the pool," he said to her.

"Craig, everything will be okay, if you're worried about me, I'll be fine. We both knew what we were getting ourselves into and I never expected anything from you," she said to him.

Craig really loved her and he wanted to be with her and only her and he was tired of worrying about his marriage and losing her for good. "Heather, you don't understand what I'm trying to say is that, I'm in love with you. You're the only one I want to be with. I know I can't be with you while I'm still married. It's not fair to anyone and now when I get my divorce, I fear you wouldn't trust me. I just wished we would have stayed friends and waited until I was divorced, then asked you out. Don't you see everything's a mess now and I can't fix it and now I'm scared I will still lose you?" Craig said to her. Heather was very shocked and speechless as she wasn't prepared to hear what all she had just heard from Craig. Now she didn't quite know what to make of it, but she did know how she felt about him. She wasn't ready to let him go either and she wasn't about ready to put her life on hold for him either.

Heather assured him not to worry so much and that they would still be together. "Craig, honey, you didn't mess anything up with us, who knows what will really happen. We will just take things day by day and see what happens. I knew what I was getting myself into and if things happen later between us, then we will work on it at that time. I will tell you this though, I won't wait for you or put my life on hold for you while you figure out your marriage. We can still see each other but I'm going to date other guys and well, if we're meant to be together then we will be," she said to him. Craig wasn't too thrilled about her going to be with other men but he couldn't tell her not to date. They finished talking and Heather went back to watching movies with Kip.

Chapter 4

Heather had been confiding to her best friend, Linda, about everything. Of course, she had advised her to stop seeing Craig that it would only lead to trouble that she didn't need. Heather was at a loss; she knew that she had to let Craig go completely and move on with her life and it was killing her inside. After Craig had heard that Heather had been involved with another man, it was making sense now why she was avoiding him. He thought there was no way that he could let him take her away. He loved her and wanted to be with her and the last thing he wanted was to lose her to someone else. Craig knew he had no right to say anything being a married man and now, he had to figure out what to do. He was also aware that she was going to date as she made that clear to him. Craig then started to put a plan together to help him figure everything out. What was going to be the hardest part of it all was his marriage and what he was going to do about it. He realized and admitted that he doesn't need to be married or deserve to until he can honor it.

Which had been very hard for Craig as he never seemed to be happy with anyone for too long. He had been married twice and two kids, one with each wife. Craig had been going crazy not knowing what to do now and asking himself where he went wrong. As Heather and Brian had been spending time together, they both realized they were better being friends. When they kissed for the first time, they both knew there weren't any real romantic feelings between them. Now, Heather had herself in one hell of a bad situation because she felt in her heart that she belonged with Craig. She just didn't know why or how this could be when he was a married man. She knew that he wasn't about to leave his wife for her and if he did, how she could really trust him.

There were so many questions that she had and she knew there was no possible way they would get answered. Her heart kept pulling her back to him and she thought why she had to fall in love with a man who she couldn't truly be with. She had gone against everything she had stood for and now was caught up in a very bad mess. There wasn't anything at all good that was going to come from this; only heartache and embarrassment if people found out. All she kept telling herself was that he would never leave his wife for her. Then if he would, how could she fully trust him not to cheat on her if they were serious. All of this kept playing in her head telling her over and over he would never leave his wife and she would be left with hurt and pain. Heather knew that she loved this man more than she had ever loved a man in such a long time. The last thing she wanted was to get herself in a trap and get her heart ripped from her chest.

As she thought more about their relationship, she realized that even though they never had to fake anything; they were never completely honest either. They both had fallen in love very quickly and failed to say something except for when Craig called her drunk. It had been a very long time since Heather had connected with anyone and felt she could be herself and not hide. Then she began to wonder why she allowed herself to fall in love with him. She knew she was playing with fire that she couldn't put out and would only burn her badly. All she could hear was his voice telling her that this wasn't something you could just turn on and off. He was falling in love with her when he said that to her. It took her until that moment to realize what he was trying to tell her. How could he look her in the eyes and tell her how he really felt when he was married? How could he expect her to believe that he wanted more than a simple love affair? Craig was hurting too just as bad as she was and something had to be done right away.

Heather was a mess, she needed to get away from it all for a while and clear her head. She decided that the only thing she could possibly do was drown herself in her work. Since she really couldn't just leave and go away with her job and all. This was something she had to face and deal with head on with Craig. Heather had to make a decision which was to finally walk away from Craig or continue to see him. Several days later, Craig had called Heather to let her know he was telling his wife about them and that he wanted a divorce. At first, she was completely in shock and was speechless.

She felt that it was best for him to think about what he had said and what he was doing. "I don't think that is the best thing for you to do right now. I'm sorry but this really has gone on too long and I feel we need to end this for now. You need to take care of this and I need to get myself together, Craig," she said to him.

Even though it was upsetting for her to do this, she also knew it was the right thing to do. "Wow…are you serious? You really want to end things and not see me anymore? Heather, I can't lose you right now, I care for you and you know that," he said to her. She knew he was hurting and was upset and she felt the same but this had to be done now.

"Craig, I understand how you feel, this isn't good for me either but if we are meant to be together, we will be. I need to know that I can trust you if or when I give you my heart completely. I can't afford to get hurt like this, not this way. I want someone I can love who can love me back fully. I'm sorry but right now, you can't give me that and it's going to take some time for me to trust you," Heather said to him.

This was not what Craig had expected to hear. "I understand what you're saying, Heather, and I'm sorry if I've made you feel like I was using you or never cared. You really do mean a lot to me and I understand now what I have to do," Craig said to her.

"Craig, you never made me feel like that and I know you care for me and I know how I feel about you, which is why I have to walk away now and let you take care of your marriage. I need to get my life back in order and if things work out for you then, great. If not…then you know where find me, if you still want me and if I'm still available," she said to him.

As he was listening to her, all he could do was cry and he felt a part of him dying inside. He had to do something now before he lost her forever, but he knew he couldn't do it alone, he needed some help. That was the last time they had spoken or seen each other and as she went on with her life; he was making changes with his. Craig knew that he was in love with Heather and he knew she loved him. Now he needed to figure out what to do about his marriage which had been over for the last five years now. He was tired of always doing the right thing and always being unhappy and not being in love and or loved back. He was getting too old for all these games of running around trying to fill the void he was missing. He wanted to be with Heather for the rest of his life and now he had to make sure that she trusted him enough and had faith in him. So, for the next few months, he started going to counseling and he informed his wife about everything and turned out, she had been involved with a guy from her work for the past year. They agreed that a divorce was the best thing for them and that they would share custody of their daughter. It seemed as things were working out after all for the both of them.

As for Heather, she was still at the same place but she had left sports and went onto working as a newscaster. This was a great change for her, that way she wouldn't have to see Craig and she felt the career change was good. There was so much that was going on with Craig and all he wanted was to call Heather and hear her voice. Once he found out she left sports for news, he knew then how she really felt. He knew that he needed more than just a phone call to make her believe he loved her. He was going to have to not only show her but prove to her that he really loved her. His worse fear right now was that she would move on to find someone else. Maybe that would be what he deserved. He felt if she did because of how they started out in the first place. It didn't really hit him until he was sitting at a café eating when her friend Kip walked in and seen him. They began to talk about Heather and with Kip being her best friend, he knew what she went through with him. Kip had told him everything, not to be mean or cruel, but to let him know and make him see how much Heather really did love him. Kip left him with knowing that she still loves him very much and then told him that he needed to get himself together and go get her. Craig thanked him and from there, he began to work on getting things done right. It would be another two months before he was divorced but for now, they had got a legal separation until their divorce was final. Craig was on a mission to win Heather back and get his life straightened out.

A month later, Heather had started dating again as she needed to make sure herself what she really wanted. Well, Craig had gone on with getting his life back in order and he respected her space and left her alone. He felt it was for the best for them both for now to keep some distance between them. They needed this time apart and she needed to rediscover herself as well. It didn't matter where either one was, it seemed they always knew what was going on with each other. These had really loved one another and Craig had to really make sure he earned her trust as well as her love. As he kept himself busy between football and being there for his daughter, he began to rediscover who he was again. Then one night watching a movie, he realized that he could ask Heather out on a date. He thought that was the best way for them if they were to start dating one another.

What a better way for them to be together and get to know one another, he thought. Craig had decided to call her later in the week and ask her out on a real date now that he was officially able to. The question now was, would she agree to see him again after all this time. Things were different now as he had his own apartment now and legally separated and waiting for his divorce to be finalized. Heather had been keeping herself very busy and she had plans of her own. She knew how much she really loved Craig and with her living in a different city, she was concerned how it would work. She was two hours away from him which was why it was always hard for them to see each other. Heather decided to follow her heart for once and she began to put in a transfer to one of the networks in South Bend. Then as she began to look for herself an apartment to rent, she was praying that she was doing the right thing.

Well, as for Heather, she wasn't about to jump in again with Craig, she needed this time to get herself situated. She knew how easy it would be to get wrapped right back up with him and she wasn't ready for all that. As she was moving into her new place; Craig had learned that she had left and transferred to another network. Of course, with the privacy laws and confidentiality, they were unable to let him know where she had gone. This had Craig worried and not knowing what to do now. He had no clue of her whereabouts and with no forwarding address or phone number, it made it even harder for him to track her down. That was until late one night when he was watching the late nightly news and seen her on one of the local networks. He jumped from his sofa and grabbed his phone and called to see if they could give him any information on her. When they discovered who they were speaking with, they confirmed that she worked there but couldn't give out private information.

After speaking with them, he was able to find out when she worked so that he could see her and find out what was going on. Craig knew that he was on thin ice with Heather and he also knew he was taking a big chance going to see her. He felt this would be the perfect time to explain things to her and see if they could start over. Now with Heather, she wasn't ready to face him as she knew what would happen. They would take one look at one another and it would be over before anything would be said. When it came to those two, they couldn't keep away from each other and not end up in a bed. There was so much heat and passion between them and everyone that knew them knew, how they felt about one another. Heather was afraid that she would fall even more in love with him and he would hurt her by cheating with someone else. She couldn't bear the thought of getting hurt like that and she had felt horrible for allowing herself to be with Craig while he was married.

A few days later, Craig was working on some things and the more he thought about how he felt about Heather, the more he felt he needed to see her. He didn't want to lose her and that was, he feared if he stayed away too long but he didn't want to push her away either. Craig had to do something, he needed to talk with Heather and find out what to do. This was really bothering him not being able to see her and talk with her, even holding her was killing him not having her around. As he watched the sports channel and worked on last minute paperwork, he decided to go ahead and pay her a visit tomorrow. He wasn't waiting around any longer and he needed to know why she didn't call him and let him know she had moved there. It was actually upsetting to him because he thought they were still good enough to keep in touch and let one another know what was going between them.

Heather was informed that Craig had called asking about her and wanted a number where she could be reached. When she learned that he knew she was living and working there in town, she knew it was a matter of time before he went to see her. It was time for something to be done, regardless, if she was ready or not. She went about her day and worked on her notes for the news. Though, before she left that day, she let everyone know that it was okay for them to give her number to Craig. She went on to let them know that they worked together and were close business friends. Craig had gotten himself caught up in some extra work with his students and players. He was unable to make it to the news station to see her, so he decided to call and speak with her there before she had left. It was then when he called the network, he found out she had left but gave permission to give him her phone number if he were to call again.

Once Craig was given Heather's phone number, he couldn't wait a minute longer to call her. All he could think about was how much he missed her and wanted to see her. Heather had just finished her bath and was getting settled in for the night when Craig called her. When she answered and heard his voice, she knew she was right back where she was several months ago. They spoke for what seemed the longest time and after they both got everything out in the open about their relationship and where things stood between them, she said goodbye. Heather let him go that night, not really knowing what was next for them. He didn't get any real answers, all he knew was how she had felt and what she wanted from him.

That night, Craig couldn't sleep and all he did was toss and turn until 4 o'clock that next morning. He began pacing the floor and decided to get a glass of milk and watch some T.V. He couldn't stop thinking about Heather and what she said to him and he didn't want her to feel that way about him. Craig couldn't take it anymore, he needed to talk with her and let her know that he really loved her and didn't want to ever hurt her. He wanted to make her realize that she would be secure with him and could trust him with not cheating on her.

An hour later, Craig called to speak with Heather and she couldn't believe he was calling her so early in the morning. This time, she really listened to what he had to say her and she was very scared to let him know she missed him and wanted to be in his arms. Craig asked to meet with her that afternoon for lunch and she agreed to meet him. He had to win her back and make her see that he loved her and only her and wasn't about to let her go now. Everything seemed to be going great between them and they agreed to take things slow and date for now. Heather was in love with Craig and she knew it when she couldn't find anyone she was interested in. All she could think about was being with Craig and how much she had missed him.

Even now with how things were and knowing that the only reason for moving to South Bend was to be able to be with Craig. She had her heart guarded for now as she agreed to move forward with Craig. It's strange how things work all fair in love and war, as they say. One day, you can have everything you thought you wanted and be very happy and the next day, have nothing. Craig learned the hard way that by jumping into an unwanted relationship to please others or because it may be right technically isn't, when it's not what you really wanted in the end.

Chapter 5

As Heather was starting her new life in South Bend with her new job, she was wondering if she had done the right thing. She thought to herself, was it really all worth it to have left her home and friends for a man who may not really love her. Heather had begun questioning herself, was she doing the right thing here? Or was she making an even bigger fool of herself for thinking and hoping that Craig just might actually love her. However, despite all of her fears, she still loved him and felt he was the only man she could ever love.

Actually, Craig was not so good as he began to really look back at his life. It was time for him to rediscover what made him the way he was and if he could stop. He didn't want to continue living this way being in unwanted marriages and living the lifestyle he had been. The question now was really knowing how he felt for Heather and if he loved her or did he love the idea of her. Then as he thought about her while pacing around his living room, something beyond was telling him he was meant to be with Heather. Of course, this wasn't good enough for Craig, he needed to know for sure and he needed to prove to Heather that he really did love her.

Here, Craig was now fifty years old, two divorces and two children to show for. No doubt he was also a great assistant college football coach with a very nice lifestyle, but it was never enough for Craig. It seemed that no matter how hard he tried staying faithful to his marriages, he always found his way in another woman's bed. Craig sat there on the sofa, closed his eyes, and began to think about his life and how he got to be who he was today. He wasn't too happy with himself and as the night got later and darker, he wasn't getting the answers he was hoping for. This wasn't as easy as he had thought so he left it alone for the night.

It seemed that even though he was done, his mind wasn't and as he drifted off to sleep, his dreams took him where he needed to be. With so much worry weighing on his mind and heart, his mind took him back in time. Craig woke up hours later drenched in sweat from the dream he was having and it was then he realized, he needed help. He needed to speak with someone about what he was going through. Just whom had he thought as he didn't know who he could turn to with this. This was something very serious and not to be taken lightly, he needed real help with this. So, later that week, Craig had decided to speak with a psychiatrist about this. Over the next several weeks, Craig began to see a psychiatrist to help him with what he was going through. It hadn't even occurred to him that he hadn't heard from Heather at all either. Craig was too busy wrapped up in trying to get some help. He needed to find out if he was even meant for real love.

He wanted to be loved and to love back, not continue playing games and dating multiple women. He knew he didn't want to spend his life alone but every time he got with someone serious, something made him cheat or not commit. Though, not with Heather at least, not wanting to cheat on her. Being with her and being away from her only made him love her more. This was what he couldn't understand why he did cheat with everyone else; but with Heather, he didn't and she made him want to be a better man. Craig realized that he needed to take care of himself first before he could be with Heather. As he went on to focus and tried to remember what had made him, who he had become, he was feeling very depressed. All of a sudden, he didn't like himself at all and then he was informed that it wasn't entirely his fault. It wasn't all completely his fault. Could he have prevented some things from escalating to the point of ending the marriages? Why of course.

As he went on to continue thinking about things, he realized maybe he never really loved either one of his wives. Craig was young and a player back then and wasn't interested in being serious with anyone. As he thought about it more, the one thing he did wrong was the one thing he was always told was the right thing to do. Which was after he had dated his first wife, she had gotten pregnant and he stepped up to do the right thing and married her. Then he thought maybe she had felt the same at the time and felt it was for the best to get married for the baby. They were both miserable but happy at the same time working and being a family. They were both working towards their careers and getting themselves accomplished.

It wasn't easy for either of them and after cheating on her with who later became his second wife, he knew it would soon be over. Craig began questioning his actions and everything he had done up until now. He didn't know what to do at this point, he felt as if he really messed up his life. All he could see was Heather right now and even with all the hurt and failed relationships, he didn't want to lose her. What would he have to offer Heather now, other than a head full of worrying that he may cheat on her just the same? He needed to get his life straight and show her that she was the only woman for him.

This wasn't going to be easy because she already knew what he was about. She had even told him that they would never make it in a serious relationship because she couldn't trust him. To not to be trusted and loved by her was destroying him and for the first time in his life, he felt useless. Then while meeting with his friends for lunch one day, they all were talking about his situation. One of his friends had questioned the fact if she didn't really love Craig, then why change her life around? Why move and relocate your job if you don't love someone and want to be with that person? There, it was the big questions that Craig needed to hear and he already knew the answers to them both. Craig knew that Heather really loved him and he knew that she also knew he loved her very much. With these two loving one another wasn't the issue, it was the matter of the heart and trusting it.

All Craig knew was that he didn't want to waste any more time being out of love and being alone and miserable. As they all talked about the good times, they all had; Craig couldn't help to remember last winter. He had reserved the cabin for the weekend of one of their games. They were in Michigan at the time and the place was nestled on the lake. It was so amazing and the snow was decorated everywhere. He smiled as he remembered them playing in the snow having snowball fights and him tackling her gently to the ground. They had so much fun that weekend and he could still feel her somehow, even now. Everyone who knew them could see how much they were in love with one another. It had become so obvious between both their friends and even strangers.

The more that Craig looked back at the time they shared together, the more he seen how much of a fool he had been. He realized that the first time he had told Heather he loved her was when he was drunk. Damn, he thought how stupid was he for that, why did he have to tell her that while he was drinking? Then he tried very hard to think back if he had said it again after that or had time passed before saying to her again. Craig couldn't remember too much, all he knew was that he didn't just love her; he was deeply in love with her and needed her in his life. Not just for a week or two or every once in a while, no, he wanted her for all times. He knew there was something special about her the first time he met her. Then years later, meeting again at that bar seeing how beautiful she looked, he couldn't explain it, he just knew he loved her and she was supposed to be with him, nobody else.

Several days later, Craig had hit rock bottom, he fell so far, he couldn't take it any longer. He was hurting and aching for Heather and as he sat at home alone, all he could was cry and feel sorry for himself. Then the following night, he had pulled himself together, got cleaned up and went to see Heather. Although, when he walked up to her front door step, something made him stop. He wasn't quite sure if she would speak to him, if she was even ready to see him or even cared anymore. She stopped calling him and wouldn't return his calls either, so he really didn't know what to expect at this point from her. Craig decided to just walk away and leave as he didn't know if she had company or even moved on with her life. He felt he had already lost her and couldn't blame her, if he did because how could she ever trust him. He cheated on his wife with her and even though she had gone along with it, she knew or felt it wouldn't last.

Her words kept playing in his mind about how she could never trust him to be seriously involved with him. How she told him that she had a lot of fun with him and then he remembered when she allowed herself to get too close. As he sat there on her steps, he remembered seeing her old friend at a diner and listening to him tell Craig how much he hurt her and that she really loved him. How could he be this bad of a person, he thought to himself. Maybe he shouldn't be with anyone. Even with him feeling that way, he didn't want to live his life that way. Here he was scared of losing the one woman who for the first time in his life he really loved.

Craig had been divorced for a short while now and Heather knew that he was. That had made him think that maybe she was right all along but then why move to South Bend? And go to work for another network station and leave sports if she didn't really love him. Something just wasn't making sense to him and he needed answers now. Craig then stood up and walked up to her door and began to knock on her door and hoped she would answer and speak with him. Craig left that night with no answers and not seeing Heather either as she didn't answer that night. He had later found out that she was gone out of town for a news conference.

It was a few days later that week when Heather had finally called Craig. She had heard about him sitting outside her apartment, waiting for her and she questioned him. He admitted that he was there and was hoping to speak with her and then he let her know he missed her. She had informed him that she had been extremely busy with work and was in several different training and conference meetings. That seemed to make him feel somewhat better knowing she wasn't ignoring him on purpose. They spoke for a while and then she agreed to see him once she was done with everything. She had so much going on that she couldn't afford any distractions but did make it clear to him she wanted to see him which had made him feel much better and put his mind at some ease.

It was true. Heather was very busy as she said and she also had so much other things going on more than she could let him know. What she failed to tell him was that she was several months pregnant with his baby. She was already showing and had decided to keep the baby and raise it. She was not about to tell him and only have him want to be with her for that reason.

She deserved better and so did her baby, and there was no way that she was going to allow Craig to hurt them the way he did his other wives and children. This was why she kept refusing to meet with him and now as it was getting closer to having the baby, she felt that as he was the father, he had the right to know. She was still very much in love with Craig and couldn't allow herself to get hurt by him even though she knew it was her own damn fault. It had just felt different with them by the way they connected with each other and how they never had to fake anything. The only thing with them was getting involved while he was still married that ruined any chances of her trusting him.

A few weeks later, Heather was out shopping and didn't realize one of Craig's buddy was there, he noticed her and could tell she was pregnant. He made sure that she didn't recognize him and he left quickly and went to call Craig. This had come to a surprise to him as he didn't know anything about Heather being pregnant and couldn't believe it. Then his friend had brought it to his attention about her always having excuses why she can't see him right now which then had made him start thinking about it and then he felt that maybe she had met someone possibly. That could be why she was agreeing to meet with him when he returned to let him know her news and to tell him she had moved on with her life.

After speaking with another friend of his, he reminded Craig that he had spent time with Heather several months ago before his divorce and that she looked a few months pregnant. He had informed him that he too had seen her walking out of a clinic a few weeks ago and that she looked good and very pregnant. This really had Craig thinking and confused if she was pregnant, then why keep it from him unless it wasn't his baby. Craig didn't think he had anything to worry about because if he was the father, then Heather would have told him. His friends had to remind him of his past marriages and why he had gotten married at the time. They both gently let him know that if he was the father and they feel that he is, she doesn't want pity. She wants him to want her and the baby for love. Then they brought it to his attention about the fact she had moved to be closer to him and changed her job. Craig couldn't believe it and as they continued talking about it; he remembered the last time he was with Heather; they didn't play it safe. He thought could it be possible that he was pregnant and that was why she moved and relocated to South Bend.

Now, he was on a mission to find out the real truth of what was going on with Heather. Craig was determined to find out he needed to see for himself and right now he wasn't taking no for answer. He told his what he planned on doing and they advised against it. They explained that if he did that, it could backfire on him and that he needed to wait and let her go to him with this. It was a very delicate mess and if he really loved her like he said he did, then he needed to allow her time. He wasn't happy with the situation but agreed with them as she did agree to meet with him after she got back home. Craig began to watch the news and tried to see if he could notice her being pregnant, but he couldn't see anything.

Craig had more things to think about now besides losing her and fighting to get her back. What if he was the father of her baby and she had been going through this all on her own. This was making him feel even worse than he already had. All he could do was just focus on his work and spending time with his daughter when he could. He had to show her that he respected her and give her time to come to him when she was ready. So, Craig had decided to back off and see what happens next. With all of this going on around him, it was making it harder for him to stay away. If only she would call him and stop fighting it, he said to himself. He missed her every day and missed the talks they had and just everything. It's now up to her and God, he told himself as he wanted her and needed her in his life.

Chapter 6

Its three weeks later, and Craig finds himself in the hospital after waking up with a very bad headache. He's very confused as he questions the nurse about how he got there. As the nurse begins to explain to him that he had been in a coma for three weeks, he starts to remember what happened. It was late at night and he was driving fast, so much on his mind between Heather and his wife and not sure what to do. He never remembered having that much fun with anyone in such a long time as he had with Heather. Then he paused with confusion as that was the last time he had seen Heather. What about everything that happened afterwards, he thought then he realized everything after that was just a dream.

As he laid there in bed, the nurses had notified his wife to let her know about his condition and being awake. Craig wanted so badly to call Heather and talk to her but he didn't. He wanted so badly to hear her voice then he felt bad since nothing really happened; but that one great night they had at the bar. All he kept seeing was that night now playing over and over again. It was raining very badly and he had been drinking not paying any attention to anything and before he knew what hit him, a truck hit him from the side and he went spinning into a brick building. He had a broken arm, cracked ribs, and caused him to be in a coma until now. It didn't make any sense to him how could he have dreamed all that up and it seemed so real. It felt real as if it all happened and now with him waking up from a coma and learning that it was just a dream.

None of this was making any sense to him and over the next several days, he had been talking with a counselor about it. He thought how could something feel so real? Only be a dream that lasted three weeks long? How could that be possible? He thought and he kept questioning everything that went on in his dream? However, he was very grateful to have recovered and be alive instead of being seriously injured or even dead. Craig was definitely very thankful for that and so was his family. He never said anything about that night and neither did his friends. Now he was ready to get back to work but that was another problem he had as his doctor wouldn't release him to work for another two weeks. They wanted to make sure that he was completely healthy and stable when he went back.

Meanwhile, Heather had heard about Craig's accident and that he had come out of the coma and was recovering. She was very glad to hear that and she wanted to send him a card or something. Though she knew it was best to wait and see when the time was right. She had been working a lot it seemed and with her situation with Kip now, she only wanted to focus on her for now. With Craig being at home recovering, he had to focus on getting his strength back. Heather knew that Craig was married so she wasn't about to read into that one night they shared at the club. They danced and had a great time as she had felt and didn't really expect it to lead into anything.

She had known Craig for many years from working with him and meeting with his players each game season. Even though they had a great time that night, she even felt something with him. There was definitely something between them two and she knew it was dangerous territory.

The End